Machines that Go Up and Down

Written by Margaret MacDonald

Picture Dictionary

cable car

chairlift

elevator

Read the picture dictionary. You will find these words in the book.

escalator

plane

roller coaster

A plane is a machine that goes up and down.
Going up is called taking off.
Coming down is called landing.

This machine is a chairlift.
It takes skiers
up the mountain.
Then it goes down again.

Escalators are machines that take people up and down.
One escalator goes up.
One goes down.

Cable cars are machines.
They carry people
up and down mountains.
One cable car goes up.
One goes down.

Elevators are machines that go up and down. People go up and down in elevators.

Roller coasters go up and down, too. They go very fast when they go down.

Activity Page

1. Draw a picture of you and your friends going up or down on a roller coaster.

2. Write a story to go with your picture. Use these words in your story:
and   are   down   going   up   we

Do you know the dictionary words?